GIVING INN
*Tales of an Innkeeper
Part 3*

KATHY BRANNING

ISBN 979-8-89526-480-5 (paperback)
ISBN 979-8-89526-481-2 (digital)

Copyright © 2024 by Kathy Branning

All rights reserved. No part of this publication may be reproduced, distributed, or transmitted in any form or by any means, including photocopying, recording, or other electronic or mechanical methods without the prior written permission of the publisher. For permission requests, solicit the publisher via the address below.

Christian Faith Publishing
832 Park Avenue
Meadville, PA 16335
www.christianfaithpublishing.com

Printed in the United States of America

Welcome back to—drumroll, please—Paradise Garden Inn! The last time we were together, I had just bought my new inn. Now after a summer full of renovations and getting Paradise Garden ready to open, we are embarking on this new adventure as empty nesters while our only child, Jessica, is off at Julliard. We are both excited and nervous to start over in New York while still running Stillwater Inn in California. We are about to experience our first holiday season on the East Coast. Now let's get started so I can share with you my adventures and the tales of an innkeeper.

Chapter 1

September is usually my favorite month; it's always full of watching the leaves change their color, the skies being painted, and people squeezing the last bit of sunny warm days before they succumb to comfy sweaters and cooler temps. September is full of celebrating, preparations, and anticipation. I would normally tell you that September is my favorite month or the year. But not this year.

Shortly after opening our new inn here in Alexandria Bay, Molly, my Bichon Frisé, got sick. I took her to the vet, and she was diagnosed with kidney disease. Her kidneys had failed, and the vet gave her weeks to live. But Molly was a fighter—she defied the odds throughout the summer and held on probably longer than she should have. Her health deteriorated, and we were unable to manage her pain. The vet advised us to help aid in ending her suffering and put her down.

I sobbed as I held her. The next moment, she crossed over the rainbow bridge, and I knew my life was forever changed.

Some people say it's just a dog. Those people just don't understand how animals can make us laugh and cry—how they make us better people in a way that no human ever could. When someone says, "it's just a dog," they have never known the pain of losing a dog. But I feel sorry for them because they have also never known the life-altering bliss of loving one.

I really struggled to make this decision, and even now, I'm burdened by the choice I made. One thing I do know is that Molly is no longer suffering. I like to believe that she's up in heaven playing with Jesus and pain-free. Before she crossed the rainbow bridge, I gave her a brief rundown of what I would like my mansion in heaven to look like. I've tasked her with being my heavenly interior designer.

It might be ridiculous to some, and I'm not sure how theologically accurate it is, but it gives me comfort picturing her preparing our mansion in heaven, fluffing the pillows, picking out paint colors and kitchen tiles, and awaiting the day she and I will spend eternity together.

I always joked that Molly wasn't actually a dog. I half believed she was my very own guardian angel sent to bring me comfort. I don't know what I did to deserve such a sweet companion, but I will cherish every memory and every moment I had with her. Her presence enriched my life, and I can't seem to figure out my life without her.

I usually live by the motto that when things are hard, it's usually good and worth it. But right now, starting our new inn, living as empty nesters, and losing my furry best friend—it's a lot. I've been caught up in the swirl, and I'm having trouble holding on. I am holding on to God as an anchor for my soul like the Word says:

> And now we have run into His heart to hide ourselves in His faithfulness. This is where we find His strength and comfort, for He empowers us to seize what has already been established ahead of time—unshakeable hope! We have this certain hope like a strong, unbreakable anchor holding our souls to God Himself. Our anchor of hope is fastened to the mercy seat in the heavenly realm beyond the sacred threshold, and where Jesus, our forerunner, has gone in before us. (Hebrews 6:18–20 TPT)

"How are you doing, babe?" Alan asks as he wraps his arms around me.

"Not great," I reply through my tears.

I turn and accept as he pulls me into a comforting hug, and I let the grief come, wave after wave of sobs. After what feels like forever, I pull away to grab a tissue as I've thoroughly soaked Alan's shirt. I look up and see his cheeks tearstained as well.

"Have you seen Jessica? I heard her come in, but I didn't see her." I ask Alan.

"She's in the kitchen baking some brownies," Alan replies. "I think she needed something to occupy herself for a little bit."

"That makes sense. Baking has always been therapeutic for me. I'm going to go check on her."

"Good idea. I'm going to go take a nap. Save some brownies for me, okay?" Alan states, visibly exhausted—at least emotionally.

"Of course, babe." I give him a quick kiss on the lips as I leave him to go find Jessica.

*****

"Hey, Jessica, you're making brownies?" I ask as I walk into the kitchen.

"Yep! They should be ready soon if you want some. I'm just making a few more batches for the guests." Jessica responds.

I survey the counter littered with ingredients, bowls, and pans.

"That looks like a lot more brownies than we have guests. We only have six people here this weekend," I add carefully.

"Well, they can eat their fill of brownies then!" Jessica snaps as she slams down the whisk in her hand.

She slumps over the counter as sobs rack through her body. I run over to her and envelope her in my arms, her body now shaking as her emotions pour out.

"Let it out, baby. Molly was so precious to our family. This is a really big hit."

I encourage her to keep crying as long as she needs while I just hold her in my arms. Although she is a full-grown woman now, this is reminiscent of when she was a child and needed the comfort of her momma's arms.

"I know she was in pain," Jessica sighs, pausing to wipe her nose on her sleeve. "But I'm so sad she's gone."

"Me too," I reply.

We sit in silence for a bit as we catch our breath, wipe our tears, and blow our noses.

"You know Jessica, one reason why losing Molly is such a deep loss was that her love was so unconditional and accepting. But it's also because so many aspects of our lives are impacted. Every single facet of life is part of the loss," I explain.

"She really did love us unconditionally, didn't she?" Jessica says.

"Yes, she did, and she was so good at showing it. I want to make sure you process this in a way that helps, okay? I know it can be easy to try and avoid the feelings because it hurts so bad, but you're doing a really good job. It's all so fresh, so let's not rush through it. Let's take it easy today, okay? Give each other loads of grace, acknowledge our grief, and give ourselves permission to express it." I advise gently.

"Okay," said Jessica with a sniffle.

"Hey! I have an idea!" I exclaim. "What if we held a memorial for Molly here at the inn?"

"That would be nice. I could bake for it! Do we still have the bone-shaped cookie cutters?" asks Jessica.

"Yes, I think we do!" I respond. "Let's grab some coffee and go sit in the library and get to planning."

"Alright, thanks, Mom. I think this is going to be special," Jessica says, with a glimmer of hope in her eyes, still red and puffy from crying.

*****

Jessica and I spend all afternoon planning a memorial service for Molly. There has been a good mixture of tears and laughter. I think, well, I hope this is a good move. I know some people might think that a memorial service for a dog is ridiculous, but Molly was more than just a dog to our family. Molly was an integral part of our everyday life. Her personality was so big; you could never ignore her presence in the room despite her tiny size. She was also sensitive and perceptive. Whenever one of us was sad, having a hard day, or sick, she wouldn't leave our side until she knew we were better. She was there through so many of our big life plans and changes. It will be difficult to navigate our day-to-day life without her. So no—to us, she was not just a dog. She was family.

"So you think we can pull all this together by Sunday?" Jessica asks.
"I do believe we can," I say with optimism.

We had thought it might be nice to hold the memorial out back in the Peace Garden, but with temps being so unpredictable right now, we think it would be better to have it inside. We plan flowers—white lilies to compliment her fur—we plan the song, the food, and the guest list.

The song I chose is very special to me. If you could have a song with your dog, this is it. I first heard this song when watching *You've Got Mail*, which makes it even better. If you haven't figured out what song it is yet, it's called the "Puppy Song," and the lyrics are so sweet and the melody is whimsical. How utterly perfect for my sweet Molly.

The Puppy Song

Dreams are nothing more than wishes
And a wish is just a dream you wish to come true
Woo, woo-woo, woo
If only I could have a puppy
I'd call myself so very lucky
Just to have some company
To share a cup of tea with me
I'd take my puppy everywhere
La-la, la-la, I wouldn't care
But we would stay away from crowds
With signs that said "no dogs allowed"
Oh, weee
I know she'd never bite me
Whoa, whoa-whoa, lo-do-do-do, po-doo
Weee
I know she'd never bite me
If only I could have a friend
Who'd stick with me until the end
And walk along beside the sea
Share a bit of moon with me

KATHY BRANNING

I'd take my friend most everywhere
La-la, la-la, I wouldn't care
But we would stay away from crowds
With signs that said "No friends allowed"
Oh, weee
We'd be so happy to be
together

In Loving
MEMORY OF

Mollie Brown
Family member and best friend

MEMORIAL SERVICE SUNDAY, NOVEMBER 26TH
AT TWILIGHT (5:00PM)

PARADISE INN

*****

Today, I'm barely able to contain my sorrow. I know it's only been two days, but I hear so many voices saying, "It's just a dog," "Move on," "Get over it," "Why would you have a memorial for a dog," etc. People will say and think what they will, but she was more than just a dog to me; she was my friend, she was part of our family, and I will honor her as I see fit. I shake it off and smooth out my dress before opening the side entrance to the inn.

I walk into the dining room that we set up for the service—the room is filled with fragrant white lilies. Each small dining table has a white tablecloth, a small vase of lilies, and a small framed picture of Molly. Our close friends and guests filled in to sit at each table to pay respect. The sheer presence of people in the room has me on the verge of a full breakdown. I'm moved by our community and their love and support of us—who are still newcomers in New York! If this is not confirmation that we are where we need to be, I don't know what is.

In the back of the room, Roxy and Simone set out a beautiful spread of appetizers. Some of Molly's favorites—when she got people food, that is. On displayed on serving trays, there is an array of tantalizing finger foods, including bacon-wrapped sweet potato bites, graham crackers with peanut butter, tiny cocktail weenies, steak and burrata crostini, and peanut butter cookies—a very nice balance of sweet/savory and fancy/simple.

"Hey, Mom," Jessica says as she comes up and wraps her arms around my waist.

"Hey, babe. It looks beautiful, doesn't it?"

"It is. I'd like to think Molly would love all this attention. The diva that she was," Jessica says with a giggle.

"Oh yeah!" I exclaim. "Especially the food."

"Are you ready to start?" I ask, looking at my watch. "It's just about 5:00 p.m."

"Yeah, will you go up with me?" she asks me.

"Of course." I grab her hand, and we make it to the front of the room.

"Thank you, everyone, for coming out this twilight to honor the memory and life of Molly Brown. As you know, she was more than just a six-pound Bichon/Maltese pup. She was an integral part of our family—a companion and friend. If you were lucky enough to meet Molly, you were greeted by a lick at your ankle and a smile looking up at you, eagerly awaiting acknowledgment and affection. Molly loved meeting all the new and old people who stayed at our inns—both Stillwater and Paradise Inn. She loved her daily walks to greet everyone; we called them Molly parades as she loved being the center of attention and captured the hearts of many with her sweet and sassy disposition. Now I'd like to turn it over to my mom, but first, I have a poem I'd like to read:

Paw Prints

Left by you…
You no longer greet me,
As I walk through the door.
You're not there to make me smile,
To make me laugh anymore.
Life seems quiet without you,
You were far more than a pet.
You were a family member, a friend, a loving soul
I'll never forget.
It will take time to heal
For the silence to go away.
I still listen for you,
And miss you every day.
You were such a good companion,
Constant, loyal, and true.
My heart will always wear the paw prints of you.

*****

The rest of the memorial service is as sweet and wonderful as Molly was. It was so precious to hear our friends' and guests' stories of Molly. She was such a little thing, but her impact was big. The grief keeps coming in waves, and by the end, I can't stay standing. I have to excuse myself and go lie down.

Suddenly, I felt maybe a bit more than grief—I was not well.

Chapter 2

After the memorial, I go to my room to lie down. This is so bizarre—the pain in my body just keeps getting worse. Surely, this isn't just grief hitting my body; this must be something else. I kick off my shoes, and my feet and ankles have swollen up like balloons. My hands ache, and I can barely keep my eyes open. I let sleep overtake me, but it's a restless sleep. I toss and turn for hours with my head pounding in blinding pain until I just can't take it anymore. I call for Alan to take me to the doctor.

I'm plagued with fear and guilt. I don't know what is going on in my body, and I hate that I'm not at the inn, cleaning up and making everything run smoothly. I know I have a capable team, but I need to do my share as well.

"I hope the doctor can figure this out quickly so I can get back to the inn."

Alan eyed me with sympathy, "Don't worry about the inn right now. We need to figure out what is going on with you."

"I hate this!" I exclaimed in frustration.

Alan is disoriented and unsure of how to respond to me in such a fragile state. Alan, feeling the weight of the day, is just trying to keep me from snapping at him again until the doctor comes in.

Knock, knock. The doctor enters the room. "Hello, I'm Doctor Roberts. What brings you in today?"

I explain all my odd symptoms to Doctor Roberts as he scribbles illegible notes down on his chart.

"Let's get some blood work and run some tests. I want to check your thyroid and ANA for any possible autoimmune. We'll also check your A1C for possible diabetes." He continues to scribble in his chart. "I'll send the nurse in to do the blood work in a few minutes, and then we should have your results in two to three days."

"Thank you, doctor," I say as he leaves the room.

Alan's face looks grim as a shadow falls over it. He rubs his face in his hands and crosses his arms.

I immediately feel the weight of Alan's stress. This is not good.

The nurse comes in to draw my blood and leaves as quickly as she came. I unroll my sleeves, and we leave to head back to the inn.

Our drive is in total silence, but I can feel Alan's unhappiness as if it were a cloak draped on my back.

*****

Two days came and went. Alan wouldn't let me lift a finger. He made me stay in our room and catered to my every need. I should be grateful, but it feels like we are both resentfully just waiting for the other shoe to drop.

Finally, my phone rings. I look at the screen, and it's the doctor's office.

"Hello?" I answer.

"Hi, Mrs. Brown. I'd like you to come in and discuss your lab results. Can you come in this morning?"

"Yes, I'll be right over." I hang up and get ready as quickly as possible.

I decide to not tell Alan and just go without him; his hovering was getting old real fast, and if it was bad news, I'd rather get it on my own so I can digest it a little first without his disapproval.

Besides, it is my health we are talking about. I mean, come on. Every time I even get a cold he acts put out; I'm dreading his reaction even more than my diagnosis.

I went to let Molly out—oh, wait. And the grief is, again, rearing its ugly head. I still can't believe she's gone. Life is weird without her.

I get in the car and start the short drive to the doctor's office. I say a quick prayer under my breath and try to give all my anxiety to God. I don't want to walk in there expecting the worst. I know that whatever the outcome, God has my future in His hands. Dropping my keys in my purse, I roll my shoulders back and hold my head high as I walk into the little waiting area and let the nurse know that I'm here.

"Trust in the Lord with all your heart and lean not on your own understanding…" I repeat to myself over and over again.

"Mrs. Brown? You can come on back." The nurse walks out, looking at her clipboard. She looks up at me with kind eyes and gives me a reassuring smile. I'm sure she is very good at her job if she can make patients like me feel calm and peaceful.

"The doctor will be right in," The nurse says as she leaves the room.

"Trust in the Lord with all your heart and lean not on your own understanding…" I start repeating again.

Doctor Roberts comes into the room and goes to shake my hand. "How are you feeling today, Kate?"

"I'm okay. I guess. I'm still in a lot of pain and super fatigued."

"Kate, I asked you to come in to talk about your labs. I believe because of my findings, I can confidently give you a diagnosis. But I'd still like to send you to a rheumatologist to do a few more tests. We are looking at the likelihood of you having lupus as the cause of the symptoms you're experiencing: The skin rash, the inflammation, the extreme fatigue, and the headaches could all be signs of a lupus flare. But before we move forward, go ahead and call to schedule the appointment with a rheumatologist, and then we will go from there. Don't worry, Kate. We will find a way to help you," Dr. Roberts assured.

"Thank you, doctor." I croak out as I gather my things and head out.

As I drive home, back to Paradise Inn, I'm in shock. I don't even know how to feel or how to process any of this. I know Alan will have tons of questions, but I think I need to take a minute by myself with the Lord before talking to anyone else, even Alan. I park and go directly to the gardens in the back of the inn. I go sit on the bench swing that is draped in wisteria. I've always loved the smell of wisteria, oh, and honeysuckle! But that's neither here nor there. My brain feels like it's moving in slow motion, and everything around me is spinning.

I close my eyes tightly and whisper a prayer of help to God.

"God, help me." It's all I can croak out.

He knows my heart, He's outside of time, He knows the beginning and the end. Not even this surprises Him. I remind my heart that God still has a plan and a purpose for my life, or I wouldn't have woken up this morning. With that resolve, I pick up my phone and look through the list of rheumatologists Dr. Roberts recommended. Interesting, this one is in New York City.

That's kind of a long way to go for a specialist. Yet a long drive alone. That might be just what I need. I pick up the phone and make the call.

"Hello? Yes, I'd like to make an appointment, please."

*****

I felt a sense of calm—a piece of resolve. I look up and let my eyes hover slowly over the beauty of the garden. September has always been my favorite month—the shift in the air, the anticipation you feel knowing a break from the heat is coming. September tries its best to have us forget summer. Yet fall announces the death of things to make way for new life.

I read this quote in a magazine that has made its home in my mind:

> Another fall, another turned page: there was something of jubilee in that annual autumnal beginning, as if last year's mistakes had been wiped clean by summer.

I brought out my journal to the garden to process some of these feelings. Yet I feel compelled to sit in the stillness and let the crisp air fill my lungs and just be. I've never been one for being still. Yet here, at this moment, I can't seem to move or even find a desire to do anything else.

Suddenly, my mouth opens, and I can't help but sing. The words and melody flow out of my heart and mouth.

> Give me Jesus
> Give me Jesus
> You can have all this world
> You can have all this world
> Just give me Jesus
> I don't want anyone else
> I don't need anything else
> You are my one thing
> You are my one thing

I repeat these verses and let them sink into my spirit. Feeling refreshed and fully submitted, I head back into the inn to finish out my day by making some toffee crumble coffee cake for the guests to enjoy this evening during the social hour. It will be so nice to enjoy a freshly brewed cup of decaf coffee and some coffee cake while mingling with our guests. One of my favorite things about running the inn is meeting the people and hearing their stories. Sure, we've had our share of unsavory guests, but mostly, the people who come to Paradise Inn are wonderful. I am so grateful to be able to do what I do.

Chapter 3

October

We don't have a Dutch Bros coffee on the East Coast, but Roxy, Simone, and I have found our own little slice of caffeinated heaven here in Alex Bay (it's what the locals call Alexandria Bay). Cathy's Coffee Pot is a village staple—open year-round, thank God.

Sure, we can make good coffee at the inn, but we need a little place to escape work and fill up the coffee that someone else makes for us. Cathy's place has become just that for us.

Cathy and her husband, Nick, run Cathy's Coffee Pot together; she makes the best espresso drinks, and Nick is famous for his quiche. Not only does Cathy provide me with my much-needed espresso, but she has lived in Alex Bay her whole life, has the best stories, and not to mention, is incredibly wise. I love coming in and listening to her memories and wisdom nuggets.

"Hi, Cathy!" The three of us file in and go straight to the counter.

"We will have three pumpkin spice lattes, two with oat milk, one regular, and all with an extra shot of espresso." Simone knows our order by heart.

"Coming right up, girls!" Cathy sings over the hum of the espresso machine.

We sit down at our favorite table; Cathy always has the prettiest centerpieces. For fall, she cut the top and center out of mini pumpkins and filled them with beautiful autumn-colored mums. The smell of cinnamon and nutmeg fills the air, and Cathy brings our pumpkin spice lattes over.

"Here you go, girls, three pumpkin spice lattes. What kind of mischief are you three young ladies up to today?" Cathy asks as she sets our drinks down on the table.

"No mischief here," I laugh. "We are having a planning sesh for our first off-season. We are following your lead and staying open year-round."

"Since opening in August, we've been slammed and booked solid! It's been great, but we are pooped," Adds Roxy.

"Don't you girls worry. With that dining room of yours, you're sure to keep busy. As I always tell Nick, people never stop eating. Even when folks are cold, they like to go out to eat," Cathy assures us.

"And how are you doing, Kate? It's been a couple of weeks since Molly passed," Cathy asked with concern in her sweet eyes and care in her motherly voice.

"I'm okay. I miss her tremendously, but I'm glad she is no longer in pain. I mostly miss our daily walks and her snuggles. She left a hole, that's for sure."

"I know you loved her dearly, and she loved you as well. The risk of love is loss, and the price of loss is grief. But the pain of grief is only a shadow when compared with the pain of never risking love," comforts Cathy.

"Thank you, Cathy. That was so beautiful. I'm so blessed to be part of such a loving community. You all have welcomed us with open arms and have treated us like family after just a few short months."

I take a minute to thank God. This transition has been rough on my heart, but in His goodness, He has shown immense kindness to me.

"Alright, ladies, let's get to it!" I transition the focus to our planning sesh and pull out my planner and pen. "Now that the Inn is a bit quieter, I'm going to head down to the city tomorrow to have lunch with my friend Lynn before my doctor's appointment."

"Which one is Lynn again?" asks Roxy.

"I met Lynn a few years back. She was a guest at Stillwater Inn, and we got to talking and hit it off. She came back a few more times, and we have kept in touch over the years. Now that I'm on the East

Coast, I get to go see her. She's a social worker and works at an adoption agency in New York City."

"Oh yeah, I remember you mentioned her before. That will be so cool! Well, I'm going for a pedicure tomorrow," Simone says.

"And I'll hold down the fort while you two enjoy your day off. I'll be daydreaming about Friday and my plans with Bruce," sighs Roxy.

"What plans with Bruce?" Simone and I ask together.

"We have a date day planned. We are going for a drive to Niagara Falls, with a stop at the winery on the way home. I'm really looking forward to it. Between the kids, the move, and the inn, Bruce and I haven't had much alone time together," Roxy shared. "But let's pray for your doctor's appointment, Kate. Father God, we come to you today on behalf of my sister and bestie, Kate. Father God, be with her as she goes to this doctor's appointment. Be with the doctor and give him wisdom and discernment. But we also pray for Kate's full healing. In Your precious name, Jesus, Amen."

"Yeah, and God, we thank you that You have Kate in the palm of Your hand," Simone adds. "Thank you that you are her comfort and her healer. We just ask for your will to be done in Kate's body. In Jesus's name, Amen."

"Thank you, guys. It is tough to balance life, but man, am I so grateful to be doing this with you girls!" I gush. "Okay, now back to planning. What's next? There are no events in the village during October, just the pumpkin patch, and we currently only have a few guests on Halloween weekend."

"There is one more thing, Kate," adds Simone with a suspicious smirk.

"We are taking you on a cruise!" Roxy blurts out.

"Yep," says Simone, eyeing Roxy. "It's just us girls. We got some coverage for the inn next weekend, and we are taking a three-day cruise before you go down to Still Water Inn."

"Wow! Guys, I don't know what to say. Thank you!"

As we go back and forth, both planning for the inn, sharing as girlfriends, and planning what to pack for the cruise, I choose to focus on the gift that's in front of me. My friendship with these two women is so special. We have been through so much together through the years. We have really been iron sharpening iron for one another. Their love has gotten me through some tough times, and I thank God that He brought me such good friends.

*****

I always enjoy my drives down to New York City; time alone in the car is so peaceful. Getting up at 6:00 a.m. to make this drive is a little tough, but it's nice to be up before everyone else. I only have my needs to think about—that's different. I put on my worship music and talk to God. I definitely needed this. Even if I didn't have my doctor's appointment and my lunch with Lynn to look forward to, this drive would be worth it. I so needed some downtime in the car, alone, with God.

On the East Coast, winter is so cold, and summer is miserable unless you are inside with air conditioning or at a beach, lake, or body of water to cool off. I love the middle seasons, as I call them— spring and fall. Spring is a welcome reprieve from the harsh winters, thawing into a floral whirlwind of life. October is just perfect; it feels like a desperately needed reprieve from the heat and humidity paired with the magic of autumn's color-changing leaves. The colors are otherworldly—rich hues of burgundy, crimson, bright orange, and gold. The leaves make the trees look like beautifully adorned ladies who put on their most majestic gowns for a glamorous night out, ready to show off their finest garments.

"Thank you, God, for the beauty and splendor of your creation. Thank you for the changing of the seasons. What a beautiful reminder You have made everything beautiful in its own time, as it says in Ecclesiastes. I pray you show me the beauty and the gift that is in this season of my life, as it's so hard to see you in this sometimes. I don't want to stay in my pity party. It sucks here, and I know you have a plan and purpose for my life. I want to keep my eyes on you, no matter the circumstances. I know you are good. Your love endures all things. Thank you that You have my life in the palm of Your hand.

And thank you that You are a trustworthy Father. Be glorified by my life, Lord. I submit it all to You. In Jesus's name, Amen."

The drive into the city was exactly what I needed. I'm feeling refreshed and excited for my day. I decided to pay for an arm and a leg to park near my doctor's office since my appointment is after lunch. I can take the subway to meet Lynn at our New York City spot, Jack's Wife, Freda. It's a cute Mediterranean restaurant in Soho. I get off the Subway at Prince Street and make the short walk to the restaurant. Surveying all the people milling about the shops and streets in Soho, there is a definite style here. One of the things I love about New York City is that every neighborhood has a different feel, attitude, fashion, and culture or way of life. I find it fascinating.

I spot Lynn standing in front of the restaurant, and I wave to get her attention and stumble over one of the bricks sticking out of the cobblestone street. Just in the nick of time, Lynn runs over and helps me catch my balance.

"Whew! Thanks, Lynn! I thought for sure I was going home with a broken nose or at least a few missing teeth." I laugh to cover my embarrassment.

"No problem! I'm glad I caught you on time. Blood is so unappetizing," Lynn giggles. "Let's go get some lunch."

We walk arm-in-arm into the restaurant. "Hi, we have a reservation for two," Lynn explains to the hostess.

After checking us in, the hostess walks us to our table and hands us our menus. The restaurant is such a cute Soho staple, with flowers framing the doorway and the blue and white striped awning. They still have their outdoor seating set up, but we sit inside at our usual table for two. The waitress brings our water and takes our order.

"We'll start with some fried zucchini chips with the smoked paprika aioli," I start. "Then I'll have a kale Greek salad, please."

"I'll have the vegetable curry bowl and a side of fries, please," Lynn adds.

The waitress repeats our order back to us, grabs our menus, and leaves as we start catching up.

"How are Brad and the kids?" I ask as I take a sip of water.

"Great! Brad is settling into his role as a pastor of a church plant really well," Lynn answers. "The kids are doing well too, loving their new school. Hunter is obsessed with playing soccer, grass stains everywhere…" she laughs, "but it makes him so happy so I only complain a little. Amelia is so social; she makes friends with everyone she meets."

"So nothing new," I laugh.

"Exactly, how about you? How's the new inn? How are you and Alan adjusting to being empty nesters? How's Jessica liking Julliard?" Lynn peppers me with questions.

"How much time do you have?" I ask jokingly. "The inn is doing great. I am still in shock at how wonderful and accepting the people of Alexandria Bay have been to us and our business. It's almost like they've been waiting for us without knowing it, you know? Alan and I haven't really gotten to the empty nester bliss yet. With Molly passing, Jessica has been home more weekends than not. I mean, I get it, and I love having her home, but I want her to experience New York City and make friends at school and find a church," I add. "I definitely worry about her."

"I get it. Our kids really get into our skin, don't they?" Lynn says sympathetically.

As our food arrives Lynn clears her throat and adjusts herself to her seat, "Kate?"

"Yes?"

"I have something to ask you."

Lynn proceeds to tell me about this boy who's been in foster care for the past three years. He's ten years old, and his parents died in a plane crash. He has no extended family, and his current foster home is an elderly couple who are about to retire and are no longer going to foster. George, that's the boy's name, needs a family who can adopt him so he can have permanency and get out of foster care.

"As I was praying for George and his future parents, your face and Alan's face flashed in my mind."

So many emotions are stirring inside me as I listen to what Lynn is trying to ask.

"So will you and Alan at least meet him? If you feel good about it after the meeting, I can take him up to the bay for weekend stays and go slowly so you guys can feel it out."

"Lynn…wow…I have so many feelings, but I must be transparent with you. I'm going to a specialist for an autoimmune disease I may or may not have right after lunch, and there is a lot of tension between Alan and me, but can I say maybe?" I ask.

"Of course! Thank you for your honesty, Kate. How about this? Go home tonight and talk to Alan about it. If it's a hard no, send me a text, and I won't bring it up again. But if I don't hear from you, I'll assume y'all are still praying on it, and I'll call you in the morning to set up a time for you two to meet George."

"That feels good. Thank you, Lynn."

My head and heart are swirling as we finish up our lunch. As I head out to my doctor's appointment, I know in my heart I want this so badly. I've always wanted a son; he needs parents, we are parents; he needs love, we have love. Could George be the son I've always longed for?

"Dear Lord, please add George to the long list of things I'm trusting You for. Please heal me and help Alan and I work out our frustrations in a loving way. Help George feel Your love and comfort amid this season of unrest. Whatever the outcome, Jesus, You are enough. In Jesus's name, Amen."

Chapter 4

The stress of Molly's passing and my health has put a strain on Alan and my marriage. Walking through grief and health issues simultaneously would be too much for anyone. Although Alan wants to take care of me through it all, his stress is in the way of being able to properly care for me and is unknowingly causing me to feel more like a burden than ever. Try as I might, I can't seem to find a way to work through this. The more I try to talk through it, the more defensive he gets, and the last thing I want is to seem ungrateful.

And now, we throw George into the mix. I've got a lot to process with the Lord on my drive home from the city.

Truly, I am grateful to have a husband to take care of me while I'm healing, but to be very frank—it left much to be desired. Yet how can I ask more from a man with so much on his plate already? A husband who is feeling things so deeply and carrying things that are far too heavy? My empathy and love for this man are at war with my unmet needs and desires, then smash that together with missing my constant companion and feeling insecure about my health issues.

Logically, I know this too shall pass. But right now, it feels like it might shatter me and everything I thought I knew. The worst part is I've entered yet another crisis of faith. Before my appointment, I prayed and prayed that God would heal me. So many testimonies of miraculous healings; I fervently asked that for myself. I asked others to pray for me. It didn't happen, and now, I must discover my "new normal."

But even as I say this now, I think, *Doesn't this mean this is one of those hard things I always say will be worth it?* Maybe I can find hope in that. Maybe Alan and I will find a way to become stronger and have our marriage grow deeper and better. Maybe in the end, my faith will be stronger because, yet again, I am faced with something I don't understand and need to rely on Him for. Maybe my health will become dramatically better because of this. Maybe through this process, I've met someone who will change the trajectory of my life.

And again, I'm reminded of the following:

> My grace is sufficient for you; my power is made perfect in weakness. Therefore, I will boast all the more gladly about my weakness, so that Christ's power may rest on me. (2 Corinthians 12:9)

*****

I know I need to talk to Alan and share how I am feeling with him. We need to communicate and feel heard by one another. We need to grow past this. Somehow, someway—even if it feels impossible. When we did marriage counseling, they always talked about the importance of voicing your wants. I think I got pretty good at that until I wasn't anymore—until I got so used to taking care of everyone else that my own tank became utterly and completely depleted. How will it ever get filled again if I don't say something? The dreaded "mom guilt" rears its ugly head. What is this that makes me want to completely ignore my own needs and desires to make everyone else's okay? Oh, right. The gift from my childhood was called codependency—super.

As I pull the car into the pathway that wraps around our inn, I see the lights on in our studio. I know Alan. I know he's waiting for me to make sure I'm okay and to hear about my day. I already gave him a brief overview of what the doctor said. I have lupus. Lupus is a chronic illness that can affect many parts of the body, including joints, skin, kidneys, blood cells, brain, heart, and lungs. It's an autoimmune disease, which means my immune system is damaging my body instead of protecting it. It is not curable, but it is treatable, and my case is on the more mild side. That being said, I still serve a God who heals and will continue to pray and believe for my healing.

As I walk into the house, Alan pulls me into a tight embrace and kisses me deeply.

"What was that for?" I ask, out of breath from the kiss.

"I love you so much and just cannot imagine my life with you, Kate. I need you here with me," Alan says as he pulls me back into his arms. He lets go, grabs hold of my hand, and pulls me to the living room. "Here, let's sit on the couch. I poured you a glass of wine. Do you want a snack?"

I plop into the comfy loveseat and allow myself to accept the pampering my husband offers.

"Sure," I say as I take a sip of wine.

Alan brings a bowl of nuts over and sits beside me. "Okay, fill me in on the rest of your day. How was lunch with Lynn?"

I fill Alan in about my near fall, how Lynn and her family are, and what I ate, and then I drop the George bomb and wait for his reaction.

"I think we should meet him," Alan says confidently.

"Really?" I ask in unbelief. "Even with everything going on?"

"Kate, no family is perfect. No life is perfect. But George needs a home; he needs parents with love to give, and you and I have it in spades. We may be having our issues, but it's not going to break us. We have a solid marriage, and Jesus is the center. It makes sense to invite someone else into our family. With Jessica gone at Julliard, it would be nice to have another kid to bring up as our own. We've always known we would one day adopt; I just don't think we knew it would take this long."

"Okay. If you're sure, I'll text Lynn now. She said she could bring him up to the inn."

"Do you want this, Kate?" Alan asks.

"Yes, so much."

"Then text Lynn, my love."

*****

Simone, Roxy, and I had an uneventful flight to California, thankfully. I clutch my floppy sun hat as they usher me, giggling toward the cruise ship port.

"Here we go! Ensenada, here we come!" Roxy goes up the ramp first, followed by me being guided by Simone.

The girls head straight to the bar. "We must start the journey with mango margaritas!" exclaims Simone.

We clink our glasses just as the ship sets sail. I'm actually very excited about this trip—three days of fun and rest with my two best friends. I love that they did this so I can get my mind off everything. We immediately sign up for all three rounds of karaoke. I am sleeping in tomorrow. I'm mostly excited not to cook! I mean, food access twenty-four hours a day? I feel spoiled!

Day two of the cruise: sleep in, check! Have a large breakfast, check! Lounge by the pool with my besties, check! Now getting ready for a fun evening in Ensenada. I bring a fun, flouncy red dress, and some comfy espadrilles. The three of us find a perfect little taqueria next to a salsa club. After getting off the boat, we spot a cute little bike taxi or rickshaw; we decide we have to take it. It is such a nice afternoon; the weather is absolutely perfect, and the ocean is breathtaking. It isn't too long of a ride from the boat to the taqueria. We pay our taxi driver, and I tell him I hope his calves recover well. I'm not sure he understands, but it makes me laugh.

We are seated at a table right away, and the service is phenomenal. I order tacos, obviously. Once our food and drinks come, we inhale every morsel—as we need it after all the food on the boat, but man, you cannot beat tacos in Ensenada.

We pay our bill and head next door to dance off some of these cruise calories. We just need to make sure we are back on the boat by midnight. It is 7:00 p.m. when we start dancing, and by the time I look at my watch, it is 10:30 p.m. We head out to look for a way to get back to the boat. But once outside, it is crickets. There were no taxis, cars, or buses in sight.

"I'm going to go back inside and see if one of the waitresses can help us find a taxi or bus," I say.

Simone and Roxy stayed outside to see if any taxis came by.

When I get back into the club, I stop a cocktail waitress. "Excuse me, ma'am? Do you know where I can get a taxi or a bus back to the port?"

She just looks at me and shakes her head. Uh oh, what to do? I look at my watch, and it's 11:00 p.m. now. How did we lose thirty minutes so fast? I was starting to sweat. I returned outside to see if the girls thought of anything.

They both shake their heads as I return. Just then, in the light of a street lamp, I see three bicycles unchained, just leaning against the street light. I look at Roxy and Simone.

"No," Roxy says.

"We can leave a note!" I say.

"I mean, they didn't lock them up," Simone added.

"Fine, but if we get in trouble, it's all you two!" adds Roxy.

We bike back to the ship and make it exactly at 11:45 p.m., just fifteen minutes to spare before the ship leaves the dock.

The whole next day, we rest, nap, and lie by the pool—really only get up to eat. Then we arrive back in California. What a sweet, although short, memorable trip.

*****

Roxy and Simone fly back to New York to work at Paradise Inn; I hop on a flight up north California to check on Stillwater Inn.

Last I spoke to Nikki, she said things were running smoothly, but she needed to hire some more help. I told her I would come and help her through the interviews and hiring. Seeing Stillwater after a few or more months is almost surreal; this is where it all started. This is where the dream became a reality—where my life changed forever.

We had a lot of really qualified applicants, but in the end, it came down to fit and personality, and we found a winner; her name is Midge, and she is hilarious. Seeing her together with Nikki was like watching a bit. They were not just going to work well together, but they were going to have a lot of laughs doing it.

Time to head back to New York to meet George!

*****

It's Saturday! Today is the day—Lynn is driving George up to meet us. I'm so excited! I baked my coffee cake and my pumpkin cookies, and I made a crackle. I just want George to be excited to be here and feel nurtured by us.

Just then, Lynn's car pulls up.

"Alan! They are here."

Knock, knock.

"Hello, welcome! Come on in," Alan and I say as we usher Lynn and George inside the door.

George is short in height for a ten-year-old boy. He has a mop of strawberry blond curls on his head and a scattering of freckles on his nose. His eyes are chocolate brown with a mischievous twinkle. He's seeming a bit coy and bashful, twirling the strings from his hoodie.

"George, these are my friends and owners of the Paradise Inn, Kate and Alan Brown," Lynn breaks the ice.

"Hi, George! Happy to meet you," I gush.

"Hiya George. How was the drive?" Alan asks playfully.

"I can't drive. I'm only ten years old!" George exclaims, matching our energy.

Lynn, Alan, and I burst into a fit of laughter, and Gregory just eyes us all until his smirk turns into a full beaming smile as he realizes he caused the laughter.

"George, I hope you're hungry because I've got lots of goodies laid out and some lemonade. Are you thirsty?" I ask.

"Did you bake all this?" George asks with wide eyes.

"She loves to bake," Alan says. "And she's really good at it too."

"Yum. Can I have one of each?" George asks politely, trying so hard to keep his hands at his side.

"Of course," I laugh as I make a plate for him. "Go ahead and sit down. We can chat while we have a snack, and then would you like to walk over to the pumpkin patch?"

"Yeah, that sounds fun!" George says.

Alan and I look at each other with a knowing smile—this is fun. I know after this, we are going to ask Lynn to let him stay over the weekend. We gotta get to know this kid, but so far, even just ten minutes in, I can feel the joy that he is filling our home with.

*****

George ends up staying the night. Lynn returns back to the city to get our home study dust off and fast-track. Since we had a home study done before, she says she will be able to pull a few strings and have someone come out to update it quickly. She'll then come back Sunday afternoon for him so he can get back to school on Monday. Lynn is such a superhero and is so committed to finding the right home for the kids in her care.

George had a blast at the pumpkin patch. Alan took him on a hayride, and I helped him pick out the perfect pumpkin. We eat grilled corn and drink hot apple cider. It is like the three of us were always meant to be together—we fit so well. I know from our time as foster parents that there is usually a honeymoon phase, so I know things can change, but I just want to enjoy this moment right now.

George went to sleep tired and content in the spare room. In the morning, he comes to church with us and seems to love children's church; he even makes some friends. By the time Lynn drives off with George, Alan and I collapse into our love seat, fully tired but smiling from such a sweet weekend.

"So?" I look at Alan.

"So?" He responds.

"Are we ready for this?" I ask.

"I think we can keep praying about it, but I feel really good about George. He seems like such a great fit for our family," Alan states.

"I agree. I'm gonna see if Jessica will come home this weekend so she can meet George too. It is Halloween, and she loves getting dressed up and seeing all the cute trick-or-treaters. Maybe she would even take George around to get candy."

"I say we keep having him come for the weekends and make the decision after Thanksgiving." I decide.

"Sounds like a plan," Alan agrees.

"Babe?" I ask.

"Yes?"

"When are we going to talk about us? I would really love to maybe do some more marriage counseling."

"I know. Let's get through the next couple of weeks. November is a busy month for us, the inn, and now, with your health and incorporating George into our lives. I'm a little overwhelmed. I'm not sure I'm ready to deal with it," Alan explains.

"Should we say no to taking in George?" I ask. "If it's too much, maybe we shouldn't add anything right now."

"No, I don't think that's the answer. He needs us. And I think we need him."

"I know. But I need you. I need us to be okay," I plead.

"We are, we will be. Just give me time."

Chapter 5

Halloween

Jessica comes on the morning train since she doesn't have any Friday classes, and I pick her up from the train station. After a quick stop at Cathy's for a pumpkin spice latte, we head to the inn. I love that Jessica has become such a capable, strong, independent woman, but I also really love it when she comes home and I get to dote on her.

"Jessica's home!" I announce as I open the front door.

"Welcome home, baby," Alan pulls her into a big bear hug.

"Dad, I haven't even been gone that long." Jessica pushes Alan away but smiles anyway. "Okay, fine. I missed you guys too. What time is George getting here? I found him the cutest Spider-Man costume in the garment district."

"Oh, that's so cute!" I gush.

"That's perfect. The little guy and I had a whole conversation last weekend about his love for Spider-Man." Alan adds.

"So let me guess, you are dressing as Spider-Gwen?" I ask.

"You know it!" Jessica dramatically falls into a superhero pose.

"I've got all the candy for the trick-or-treaters, but I'm finishing up the final batch of pumpkin butterscotch cookies for the guests and starting to prep for dinner. Wanna help?" I ask hopefully.

"Sure, let me just drop my stuff in my room, wash up, and I'll be right down. That pumpkin spice latte kicked in. I'm feeling all that caffeine and sugar coursing through my veins!"

"Perfect," I add.

"I'll be in the study working if you ladies need a taste tester," Alan says before we all go our separate ways.

*****

Just as Jessica and I finish getting the cookies and cider set out for the guests, Lynn's car pulls into the drive, and George barrels out of the car and races up the steps.

"Hi, George!" I say as I open the door.

George comes through the threshold and throws his arms around my hips into a big hug. My heart melts as my eyes meet Alan's.

"Hey, buddy! How was the drive up?" Alan asks.

"It was alright. I got kind of bored, but I'm glad we are here now!" George says matter of fact.

"Lynn, Brad, thank you so much for driving him up this weekend." I turn to give Lynn a hug as Alan shakes Brad's hand.

"No problem. Thanks for having us as a guest at the inn. Such a perfect place to celebrate our anniversary," Lynn says as she looks at Brad, all googly-eyed.

"I'm just glad it worked out for my parents to keep the kids," Brad adds, not taking his eyes off Lynn.

"Well, here are your keys, you two love birds. I'll have Jessica take you up to your room, and then, if you feel like it, I'll bake some of my famous pumpkin butterscotch cookies and put out some cider and wine for the social hour," I offer.

"That sounds lovely! We may pop down for a quick treat," Lynn says, "I love your pumpkin cookies!"

Jessica takes Lynn and Brad up to their room, as we take George to his and get him settled.

"Okay, George. I bet you're hungry after that long drive! Want to try one of my cookies before dinner?" I ask.

"Yes, please!" George responds excitedly.

We go into the living room, where I put a small plate of cookies and cider for the family. Jessica is already down there helping herself to the cookies,

"George, this is our daughter, Jessica," I introduce them.

"Hi, George. Nice to meet you," Jessica says with her mouth full of cookies.

"Hi, Jessica. Are you taking me trick-or-treating?" George asks boldly.

"Yes! As a matter of fact, I even got us the coolest costumes to wear," Jessica says as she pulls them out of a shopping bag. George's eyes grow wide as he takes in the bright red spidey suit and her white and pink suit.

"I bet we get a ton of candy in those!" George exclaims.

Jessica and George chat more while I get dinner on the table, and we enjoy our very first dinner together—all four of us. I'm sure you're wondering what I made. Well, I made a family favorite: apple cider pork roast with mashed potatoes and green beans—the perfect fall meal.

*****

After dinner, Jessica took George around the island trick-or-treating. The locals love seeing children all dressed up in their cute little costumes. I know a lot of people, especially Christians, choose to reject Halloween and everything related because it can be dark and creepy. I'm not saying I'm the authority on these things, but I feel very strongly that if we are to love people, then we can't stay in our little bubbles; we must go and love people where they are. I don't celebrate death. I don't celebrate fear, but I do promote fun and try to be the light to folks wherever they are. So now, that is all I will say on this subject.

After Jessica and George hit up the houses in the neighborhood, they walk down to James Street, where the local businesses have set up a fun block party with games, face painting, and enough candy to keep the town dentist set for years. While they trick-or-treat, Jessica asks George all kinds of questions about Spider-Man and his favorite hobbies. They are chatting practically the whole way.

"What's your favorite candy, George?" Jessica asks as they head to the first booth.

"Skittles!" announces George.

George have eaten most of the candy from his pillow sack; Jessica can tell George didn't seem to have much, if any, self-control with the sweet treats. She thought to herself that she better keep a close eye on him and pray he doesn't get sick. The music is blaring on the street, and laughter fills the air, and children run around from booth to booth, getting more and more candy.

One of the booths has a fog machine running; the children near the booth seem to be having a blast running through the fog. Suddenly, a little boy kicks it hard with a bang, and the machine sputters and fills the air with dense fog. George gets so frightened by the loud sound that he looks around the street filled with fog, and he can no longer see Jessica—or anyone else, for that matter.

George starts panicking, and he feels like he can't breathe. Flight-or-fight kicks in, and George starts running—all he can think about is getting out of the fog. Surely, if he can get clean air, he will be able to find Jessica and ask her to take him back to the inn. Just then, he feels a hand reach out and grab his hand. At a moment of clear air, he sees that it is Jessica. He breathes a sigh of relief.

"You want to get out of here?" asks Jessica.

"Yes," George answers in relief.

They head down James Street in the opposite direction toward the clear air. All of a sudden, George spots a big pink sign that says The Whole Scoops.

"Hey!" George says and tugs Jessica's hand. "What's that?" He points toward the ice cream shop.

"Do you like ice cream?" Jessica asks playfully.

"Of course!" George yells.

They playfully zoom like they are swinging from webs in their Spider-Man/Gwen costumes all the way to get some ice cream.

Jessica and George come home laughing and on an obvious sugar high. They have an amazing time together, bonding. I, on the other hand, do not have such a great night. I must have overdid it. I am having a really bad flare and have to go to bed early.

*****

The whole next day, I am down for the count. Alan and Jessica take George to the movies and to the park; they handle all the food and entertainment for the weekend. When Lynn and Brad drive off with George and Jessica, they so kindly offer to drive her back to school. Alan collapses next to me on the couch and grabs the remote.

"I'm so tired," Alan states.

"I know. Thanks for hanging out with the kids this weekend. I hate that I couldn't spend more time with George this weekend."

"Yeah, you have got to stop overdoing it," Alan says, visibly annoyed. "How are we supposed to move forward if you are always in bed?"

"Wow! I don't even know how to respond to you right now, Alan. That was so uncalled for. It's not like I planned this; it's not like I chose to have lupus. This is all new to me. I don't know how to do less."

"Well, you're going to have to figure it out, Kate. I'm here to help, but it's no good if you keep shooting yourself in the foot and taking on too much."

"What was I supposed to do, not have George come? Cancel all the bookings at the inn?" I ask furiously.

"No, but did you have to bake AND make dinner from scratch on Friday? I know you were already prepping for George, but it just seemed like you took on too much. You could have just bought cookies and ordered pizza. Kids like pizza, Kate!"

"Whatever! I can't talk to you right now; I'm going back to bed. I hope you are comfy right there on the couch."

Chapter 6

November

Thanksgiving is right around the corner, but before all the holiday festivities, Alan and I celebrate our twentieth anniversary. It's hard to be excited as we still haven't gotten a chance to talk and figure things out. The tension and stress trigger and aggravate my symptoms, and then Alan gets frustrated that he can't seem to fix me, and then I get mad at him for trying to fix me. It's an ugly cycle. All I do is grit my teeth and try to keep it together—especially around George. The poor kid has been through enough that I want him to feel carefree when he visits the inn.

Jessica booked Alan and me a room at the plaza in the city and got us tickets to a Broadway show; perhaps being away from the inn will give us time to talk. Lord, please let us work this out. I am believing you for my physical healing as well as reconciliation for my marriage. George is at the inn this weekend with Jessica, doing some fun kid bonding. I know she's technically an adult, but they are my kiddos in my heart.

*****

"Ready, babe?" I ask Alan.
"I'm ready! Roxy and Simone are holding down the fort, and I've got everything I need for our weekend in the city. Let's go!" I say excitedly as I put my bag in the trunk.
"Let's finish ironing out our Thanksgiving plans on our drive," I suggest, not ready to talk about the hard things.
"Sounds good," he agrees.

"So your parents and sister are flying up. We've blocked off two rooms for them. George and Jessica are coming, and my mom and Henry, my brother, and his family are also coming. We have a full inn for Thanksgiving," I process out loud as I jot it all down in my planner and create a to-do list.

"Who's bringing what?" Alan asked.

"Since everyone is flying in, I don't want anyone bringing anything," I reply.

"You're not making Thanksgiving dinner by yourself for sixteen people," Alan said disapprovingly.

"Jessica will be my main helper, and I can give some other people some jobs, but you know I don't like too many cooks in the kitchen," I reply, getting frustrated.

Alan grips the steering wheel a little tighter and breathes a sigh of annoyance. But now I'm also annoyed—here he is trying to "fix" me again. He thinks if I do everything myself, I will have a bad lupus flare and won't be able to be fully me at Thanksgiving. I hate that I feel so controlled by not only my emotions but his as well. Jesus, help me fix this! I don't know what to do, and it makes me so sad to start our anniversary weekend in a fight with bad feelings. We have loved each other for so long, and I hate that my health has come between us.

"Do you mind stopping at the next rest stop? I have to use the bathroom," I force out.

"Sure." Alan flips on his blinker and pulls off into the rest stop. "I just don't want you making any stupid mistakes and making your health worse. It's really stressful for me."

"For you!?" I yell. "It's my health. How do you think I feel!?"

I practically fly out of the car, run into the restroom, and let the tears flow. I feel so hopeless. How are we ever going to get through this? I'm sure I'm being dramatic, but these feelings are very real for me, and I'm struggling to focus on logic and reason right now. All I know is that my heart hurts, and I'm mad. I don't even fully understand everything I'm feeling.

Dear Lord, please give me the strength to lay aside my hurt for tonight and have a good time just being with my husband. Please help me honor him despite my hurt and anger. I believe you are going to help us get through this. Please fill us with your peace that surpasses all understanding and makes our marriage stronger than ever. In Jesus's name, Amen.

I take a deep breath and dry my tears before heading back out to the car.

"Okay, I'm ready," I say as I latch my seat belt.

"I'm sorry. You okay?" Alan asks sheepishly.

"I will be. Let's drive through and grab some coffee for the last two hours of our drive," I suggest.

"Sounds good. Want to put on some fun tunes?"

"Sure."

I bring up Apple Music and start playing some of our favorite boy band music. Some silly fun is what we need right now, and Backstreet Boys and NSYNC always bring that.

"You are…my fire…my one…desire…"

We belt out as we enter the Starbucks drive-through.

"Hi! Welcome to Starbucks. Can I take your order?" The barista asks through the tiny box.

"Hi. We'll have a grande iced americano with sugar-free vanilla and a splash of oat milk and a grande white mocha," Alan orders into the speaker.

The coffee and the music help change the mood for the rest of our drive to the city. We pay an exorbitant amount of money to park our car in the hotel's garage and take our bags up to our room. We have dinner at our favorite Italian spot, Norma-Gastronomia Siciliana restaurant, and then go to the 8:00 p.m. show of *Moulin Rouge*. I'm excited to get up to our room and freshen up.

*****

Even though I have mixed feelings about Alan right now, I always love a reason to get dressed up and go out. I finish curling my hair, winging my eyeliner, and applying my bright red lipstick. Old Hollywood glamor that's what I call this look. I smooth out my Kate Spade little black dress and slide on my black boots. Now to accessorize, and I'm ready to go. As I'm grabbing my date night purse,

Alan comes out of the bathroom in his dark navy blue suit, smelling wonderful and looking tall and dashing. I feel my anger toward Alan melting just a smidge. Dang! Why does he have to clean up so good?

We take an uber to the restaurant because Alan refuses to deal with driving and/or parking in the city. We both order our favorite: the lamb ragu, bruschetta, and a bottle of Benanti "Serra della Contessa." Our food comes rather quickly, and we eat mostly in silence, aside from a few niceties. It's hard for me to ignore the tension in the air. As our meal comes to an end, they bring out a surprise anniversary tiramisu; something about the sweet gesture from a place that means so much to both of us has me yanking my napkin to keep my tears from making a mess of my expertly applied makeup.

I look over at Alan, and he's staring at me with so much love in his eyes.

I take a deep breath as I'm overwhelmed with emotion for him, the situation, the fact that we've made it after being married twenty years. It's hard, but I know it's worth it.

"Alan," I reach out and put my hand on his. "Let's figure this out. I can't go on like this. It feels like my heart is in a blender."

"Okay, Kate. You start," Alan answered hesitantly, never being a fan of conflict.

"To start, I feel so overwhelmed by this medical diagnosis. I think I've always had this superwoman complex, so being told my body has decided I can no longer operate as a superhero is shaking my identity. I know that you and Jessica have come to rely on me for certain things and are used to my being able to carry a huge load, but things have to change."

"That's what I keep trying to tell you, Kate. You are doing too much, and you're still trying to do too much, and it's going to make you worse if you don't stop." Alan interjects.

"Can I finish?" I say flatly.

"Yeah, sorry." Alan pays the check and helps me put my coat on as we head outside.

"I need help. I don't know how to ask for help. I don't know how to rely on others for things. I need a learning curve and to learn how to slow down. You can't expect me to automatically be able to seamlessly switch from doing everything to doing nothing. That's just not how it's going to work."

"You're right, Kate. I'm sorry. I didn't see that. I'm just so scared. When I didn't know what was wrong, I thought the worst, and the thought of losing you is just paralyzing."

"So in the fear of losing me, you've pushed me away. Feels like your approach has some major flaws. Despite living in the same house, we've been a million miles away from each other."

"I just want you well," Alan says, deflated.

"I do too, but I need us to be in sync as well. Let's be on the same team. Despite being in each other's lives, we haven't been present in each other's lives. It's like…we see each other…"

"But we stopped seeing each other," Alan interjects.

"Exactly," I agree.

"Listen, we can talk about what we did or didn't do right, but at the end of the day, I just miss you," Alan says as he softly caresses my cheek with his thumb. "I miss my wife."

"I miss you too," I choke out with emotion.

He kisses me deeply yet tenderly.

"Let's not miss each other anymore, okay?" I say as I rest my head on Alan's chest.

Alan wraps his arms around me. "And let's promise to be present for each other."

I give a little nod and nuzzle into Alan's embrace, not just to show my affection but to ward off the winter chill.

Just then, the first sparkling flurries of snow start to fall and swirl around us. Like our very own white winter show, I was sure that God gave that as a gift to celebrate our reconciliation.

We both lift up a prayer of thanksgiving, acknowledging God's presence and goodness in our lives.

"Shall we take a horse-drawn carriage to the theatre?" Alan suggests, knowing full well that I can't resist fairytale romantic gestures.

"How about we take the horse-drawn carriage back to the plaza and listen to the soundtrack in our hotel room?" I arch my eyebrow.

Alan knows exactly what that eyebrow means. Making up is so sweet.

Chapter 7

December

Jingle bells and mistletoe are going up all around me. Christmas music is blaring, and all the window fronts along the main street look like Santa threw up. The little village of Alexandria Bay is exploding with holiday cheer as the rest of the world is out doing their black Friday shopping.

Despite Alan and me making up and working through our issues, I've got a bad case of the bah humbugs. I usually love Christmas time, and you will think that living in such a Christmassy village, I'll be able to get into it, but I just can't seem to get out of this funk.

Thanksgiving is uneventful. Everyone loves meeting George; the families are on their best behavior, and everyone pitch in, so I don't carry the load alone. I'm learning, very slowly, how to ask for help, and even slower, I'm learning that it's okay to receive help. I think it's going to be a long road to get over this learning curve. I just wish I could figure out how to be happy again. No, not happy, joy. I want to be joy-filled. Happiness is circumstantial. Joy, true joy, can stand no matter the circumstance. Joy is fruit.

> But the Holy Spirit produces this kind of fruit in our lives: love, joy, peace, patience, kindness, goodness, faithfulness, gentleness, and self-control. (Galatians 5:22)

If I'm honest, I'm not seeing many of these fruits in my life.

What have I been cultivating these past few months instead? Fear, despair, hopelessness? I need a reset.

I think of Psalms 16:5–11 and make it my prayer:

> Lord, you alone are my inheritance, my cup of blessing. You guard all that is mine. The land you have given me is a pleasant land. What a wonderful inheritance! I will bless the Lord who guides me; even at night my heart instructs me. I know the Lord is always with me. I will not be shaken, for he is right beside me. No wonder my heart is glad, and I rejoice. My body rests in safety. For you will not leave my soul among the dead or allow your holy one to rot in the grave. You will show me the way of life, granting me the joy of your presence and the pleasures of living with you forever. Amen.

Thankfully, everything is covered at the inn for the next few days. I have a plan with Alan that he will navigate and delegate for me while I spend today and tomorrow processing with the Lord. Praying, resting, and figuring out what my new normal needs to look like, and above all, how to restore my joy.

I'm not ashamed to say I've got a hair appointment and a massage booked. I have plans to take a bubble bath with Epsom salt, candles, and tea. The next two days will be productive self-care. Wow, that's a mindset shift for me to do self-care and not feel like I'm being lazy or wasteful. This is going to be a beautiful thing! Between spending time in prayer and planning my self-care Sabbath days, I'm already feeling my bah-humbug crankiness fade away. I finish my cup of coffee and go get ready for my massage. This is going to be a good couple of days. Maybe even a good Christmas.

*****

Two weeks have gone by since my self-care Sabbath. Resting and coming up with a plan and not feeling like it was me against the world that helped lift my spirits. The Lord helped me find my joy, and now, when I need the reminder, I know that the joy of the Lord is my strength and that real rest is incredibly important and life-giving.

Since I get a boost of energy, I can finally finish decorating the inn for Christmas—a bit later than I had hoped, but I get all seven trees put up and decorated, and even with the help of Roxy and Simone, it is no small feat! Each tree has a different theme. The tree in the entryway is a local fir decorated with classic streams of popcorn and cranberries, and with decorations I collected from the local shops here in Alex Bay, this tree represents the town. In the sitting room, next to the fireplace mantle that is draped with real greenery, is another fir tree; this one is decorated with a Nutcracker theme—sugarplums, ballerinas, a rat king, and, of course, a nutcracker prince. I can just picture families sitting in this room with their children looking wide-eyed at this glorious tree.

The other five fir trees are placed in each of the guest bedrooms of Paradise Inn. One is decorated like a winter wonderland, lightly flocked with a dusting of fake snow and decorated in pearly white and different shades of blue. I found these adorable snow globe ornaments at Hobby Lobby that complete the tree.

In the family suite, we have the candy-themed fir tree dressed in vivid colors and candy-shaped ornaments. This room is definitely full of whimsy.

In the third room, we have a more rustic, naturally decorated fir tree. Ornaments made of dried orange slices and cinnamon sticks; this tree might just be my favorite because of how wonderful the room smells.

Our fourth room has a classic red and green fir tree with accents of gold and silver, old-fashioned candles (artificial, of course), and a beautiful vintage angel perched at the top, watching over our guests as they sleep.

In the fifth and final guestroom, since the window gives a direct view of the water, I make this fir tree coastal themed, with shades of aqua, white, and sand. I found nautical ornaments like sand crabs, sea horses, fish, and octopus.

Why are all seven real fir trees and all topped with angels, you ask? Because of this sweet story I once read:

> How the Fir Tree Became the
> Christmas Tree by Aunt Hede

This is the story of how the fir tree became the Christmas tree. At the time when the Christ child was born, all the people, the animals, and trees and plants were very happy. The child was born to bring peace and happiness to the whole world. People came daily to see the little one, and they always brought gifts with them.

There were three trees standing near the crypt, and they wished that they too might give presents to the Christ child.

The Palm said, "I will choose my most beautiful leaf and place it as a fan over the child."

"And I," said the Olive, "will sprinkle sweet smelling oil upon his head."

"What can I give to this child?" asked the Fir, who stood near.

"You?" cried the others. "You have nothing to offer him. Your needles would prick him, and your tears are sticky."

So, the poor little Fir tree was very unhappy, and it said, "yes, you are right. I have nothing to offer the Christ child."

Now, quite near the trees stood the Christmas Angel, who had heard all the trees had said. The angel was very sorry for the Fir tree; he was so lowly and without envy of the other trees. So, when it was dark and the stars came out, the angel begged a few of the stars to come down and rest upon the branches of the fir tree. They did as the Christmas angel asked, and the fir tree shone suddenly with a beautiful light.

And at that very moment, the Christ child opened his eyes – for he had been asleep – and as the lovely light fell upon him, he smiled.

Every year people keep the dear Christmas child's birthday by giving gifts to others. And every year, in remembrance of his birthday, the Christmas angel places in every house a fir tree covered with starry candles. It shines for the children as the stars shone for the Christ child.

The fir tree was rewarded for its meekness, for to no other tree is it given to shine upon so many happy faces.

*****

Paradise Inn is fully booked. All five rooms are full of wonderful people who come to Alexandria Bay for our Santa River Festival and the annual Swim with Santa event.

The 1000 Island River Sana Festival is a community event put on by volunteers across Northern New York. The goal of the event is to reach out to every child along the river and every child in need from anywhere in Northern New York. When Santa arrives at the village dock in Alexandria Bay by boat with a coast guard escort, he will be bringing gifts purchased with donations and sponsorships.

I'm extra excited about this event now, mostly because George will be here. It's getting harder and harder to let him go back to the city on Sunday afternoons. I know Lynn said it would most likely be by spring that our home study would get approved, but I'm praying for a Christmas miracle.

Jessica had to stay at school this weekend, and Lynn was busy, so Alan went into the city to pick up Gregory this morning, and I'll drive him home on Sunday. I have cookie dough chilling in the fridge and plan on rolling out Christmas cookies tomorrow after the Santa event. I'm so excited to share our tradition of Christmas movie night with George. We call them snowflake Saturdays. When Jessica was a little girl, they were on Mondays, and we called them magical merry Mondays.

"Honey, we're back!" Alan announced as he came through the door with George, who was oddly quiet.

I wipe my hands on my apron and come out to give them hugs. As I hug George, I can tell something was bothering him. I pull him over to the sofa and sit with him.

"Is anything wrong, George?" I ask. I look up at Alan for some hint, and he just shrugs his shoulders.

"I dunno."

"Okay, buddy, but if you want to talk, we are happy to listen, okay?"

"Can I go play outside?" George asks.

"Sure! I'm working on dinner. Alan will come let you know when it's ready, okay?"

George takes his backpack to his room and runs out to the back garden.

"He barely said a word on the drive, Kate." Alan fills me in as he follows me to the kitchen.

I stir the pot and put the lid back on. I pull out the ingredients for George's favorite, my toffee coffee cake, and finish making the dumplings for the chicken and dumplings that we are having for dinner. After I drop the dumplings into the soup and cover it back up, I start the coffee cake.

"Alan, I don't want to take him back to the city."

"Do you want me to drive him back on Sunday?" Alan asks.

"No. That's not what I mean. I'm done with the back and forth. He belongs with us permanently. He needs to be a Brown, officially."

"Oh." Alan comes and puts his arms around me, "I get it. I feel that way too. But what are you going to do? We have to wait for our home study to get approved."

"Why do you have to be so logical and practical?" I ask as I bury my head in his chest.

"So you can be our whimsical dreamer," Alan responds as he kisses the top of my head.

It's been so nice to be back connecting with Alan. We felt so far away for so long there that it was scary. Now it seems like we are back in tandem. Our anniversary really marked us and breathed new life into our marriage. It makes the hard things a little less hard.

*****

Saturday morning, after a few hearty helpings of my toffee coffee cake washed down by a tall glass of milk, George is all bundled up and ready to head over to James Street for the River Santa Festival.

Despite the chilly weather, we decided to walk over instead of drive, as the parking would be crazy today with all of the out-of-towners. George, being a city kid, is used to walking. Alan and I, on the other hand, could probably use a little more walking in our lives.

The first thing George wanted to do was go to the face painting booth. As we approach James Street, he bolts over to hop in line. Alan follows him as I hop over to Cathy's for some hot chocolate for the boys and a hot apple cider for me.

By the time I get our hot beverages, George comes running over to proudly show me his snowman on his cheek, and Alan turns to show me his matching cheek. I compliment and gush over their adorable face paintings while I distribute their hot cocoas. Next, we go over to hop on the hayride. Boy, am I glad to be wearing multiple layers, not just to protect from the cold but to shield my legs from that itchy hay.

While on the hayride, we can see Santa's boat heading towards the dock. George is so very excited to see Santa. In his words, he knows Santa isn't real, but it's still super fun to play make-believe. This is one of my favorite things about George—he can find joy in anything. He inspires me to see goodness wherever I go, no matter what it looks like.

The end of the hayride lets us off right at the end of the line to see Santa. George is ready, so in line, we go. And we wait. Lord, help me have patience. I've never been one for lines, but especially not at forty-two, in the blistering cold, waiting for kids to sit on Santa's lap. Oh well. Find the joy, find the joy. I squeeze the hands of my two guys and look out beyond the river to Boldt Castle. My goodness, we live in such a beautiful place.

To think, just a few years ago, we were living in Northern California, running Still Water there. I was living the dream, and I thought it stopped there. Never did I imagine I'd be moving to the East Coast to open a second inn and adopt a son. I've always wanted a son. I just didn't think it was in the cards for me. Alan and I were only able to conceive once, so after Jessica turned twelve, I sort of gave up on ever having another child. But here we are—my dreams gave birth to new dreams. That is enough joy to fill my heart and overflow. Thank you, God, for this beautiful gift. Now please, God, give me a Christmas miracle and let George become a Brown sooner rather than later.

After all that contemplation and silent prayer, we are finally up next. George lets Sally, who's playing the elf, escort him to Santa, who is played by old man Harley. George sits on the arm of Santa's chair.

"Listen, Santa, I know you're not real, but I know that you pray. See that nice lady over there? That's Kate Brown, and the guy next to her that's Alan Brown. I want them to be my parents. See, my parents died when I was little, and I've been in a boy's home in Brooklyn since. It's alright, I guess, but when I'm with Kate and Alan, and I guess Jessica too, I feel really good. I really like it when I come here on the weekends, and I get really sad when I have to leave on Sundays. I guess what I'm trying to say is, if you wouldn't mind, could you please pray and ask God if he could make it so I could stay with Alan and Kate and that they would be my parents forever?"

Harley was so overcome by emotion by George's request that he had to take a moment to compose himself.

"Santa?" George asked in concern.

"Well, George, I will pray for you and the Browns. They seem like such nice people, and you seem like a good little boy. I do pray everything works out for you, truly. Now what about a special toy?" Harley asks.

"Nah, toys just get stolen or broken in the boy's home," George shrugs. "Santa? Can you add one more thing to your prayers?"

"Of course," Harley responded.

"It's Kate. She's sick. She tries to act like everything is fine, but sometimes, I can tell she's in a lot of pain. I've overheard Alan call it something like lupus. I don't know what that is, but the pastor at church said that God heals. So I was wondering if you could ask him to heal Kate too?"

"Yes, George. I will pray that God heals Kate. Now you keep being a good boy, okay?" Harley says as George jumps down.

George doesn't know, but Alan and I overheard his request to Santa. I was so overwhelmed with emotions that I ran into Kelly's ice cream shop to cry in the bathroom. What was it about Whole Scoop that made someone want to run in for comfort? It could be the sugary sweet ice cream they serve, but I'd say since getting to know the owner, Kelly, it's her sweet, safe, pastoral heart that provides comfort for a hurting heart.

Knock, knock. "Kate? Is everything okay?" Kelly asks at the bathroom door.

With a wad of toilet paper in hand, I open the door and usher Kelly into the one-person bathroom. Through messy sobs, I share what I have just overheard paired with my own very deep feelings about both things.

"Oh, Kate, that is a lot all at once. Let me pray for you," Kelly says as she wraps her arm around my shoulder.

"Thanks," I sniffle.

"Father God, we ask that you come and comfort Kate in this moment. Thank you for bringing George into their lives. We ask you to make a miracle and bring this boy home with the Browns for good and answer George's prayer quickly. And Jesus, you know what's going on in Kate's body. I declare your healing over her body in Jesus's name. Thank you that you paid for Kate's healing on the cross. We submit these things to you, God, and say have your way in Kate's life. In Jesus name, Amen." Kelly finishes her prayer and gives me a sisterly hug while I let the tears flow until they run out.

"Want a scoop of peppermint ice cream? On the house?" Kelly asks.

"You get me," I laugh.

We head out to the store front, and she goes behind the counter to get my scoop. Just as she hands me the cup, her boyfriend, Kyle, walks in. I step aside and enjoy my peppermint ice cream as Kyle pulls out a small, beautifully wrapped present and presents it to Kelly.

"I got you a new ornament for your tree," Kyle states nervously.

I should go find my boys, but I'm drawn to watching the interaction between this sweet couple, as if I'm the live audience for a real-life hallmark movie. Kelly opens the wrapping paper to reveal a sterling silver angel with "Kelly, will you marry me? —Kyle" engraved in the center with a red ribbon on top to hang from the tree. As she processed what she read on the ornament, Kelly looked up to see Kyle getting down on one knee and pulling out another box—this time open and containing a gorgeous, sparkling, princess-cut engagement ring. Kelly ran around the counter and practically yelled out, "Yes!" as Kyle stood up and quickly slipped the ring on her finger before pulling her into a loving embrace.

Looks like there's going to be a wedding. What a perfect match. Kyle, the town pediatrician, and Kelly, who owns the best ice cream shop in town—their kids will be set. What a sweet moment to witness. Now that I've got a dose of sugar and a dose of sweetness from that beautiful proposal, I think it's time to go find my boys so we can head home and make Christmas cookies. I throw a quick wave toward Kelly and Kyle as I toss my empty cup in the trash on my way out the door.

Feeling a renewed sense of hope, I grab my boys from the ring toss booth, and we make the short and cold walk home. Those cookies aren't going to make themselves.

Chapter 8

Christmas week is here! We were able to arrange for George to stay for the whole week and weekend since he doesn't have school until after the new year. Between the inn being solidly booked all month, the kids being home, and the regular holiday hullabaloo, I've been extra tired. Today, I promised Alan I would take a self-care day. I really can't complain since I was able to sneak in another massage. These once-a-month massages make me feel slightly guilty, but the way my body feels so restored after makes it almost a necessity, although still a luxury.

After running to the bathroom right after my massage (releasing all those toxins), I get dressed and turn my phone on. I have twelve missed calls from Lynn! Oh man, I hope everything is okay. I head to the car, turn it on to heat it up, and call Lynn back.

"Kate!" Lynn answers before the first ring.

"Lynn, what is it? Is something wrong?" I ask.

"No, quite the opposite. Are you sitting down? Because you shouldn't be. You're going to want to jump up and down!" Lynn says excitedly.

"Spit it out, Lynn. What is it?" My heart is racing.

"You ready? You're approved, your home study. You're adopting George! Not only that, but he gets to stay with you now until your adoption is finalized. You'll just technically be fostering him."

"Really?" I ask in disbelief. "We don't have to take him back to the boy's home ever again?"

"Never again," Lynn says. "Except maybe to get his things and say bye to his friends, but only if he wants to. I'm happy to bring his things over this week or after Christmas."

"Well, let me talk to Alan. I think this would be so fun to tell George Christmas morning."

"Oh, he will love that! Kate, I'm so happy this worked out. I knew you guys needed each other. God works everything out for good, doesn't He?" Lynn says.

"Yes, Lynn. He certainly does." I hang up and call Alan.

"Babe! Guess what?" I say.

"What?"

"We get George. Now. Forever."

"What?" Alan asks. "Really? That quick?"

"Our home study is approved, and we can foster him until the adoption is finalized. We never have to take him back to the city again."

"Well, this calls for a celebration!" Alan is always wanting to celebrate.

"I had a thought, though. Let's tell him Christmas morning."

"Oh, that's such a great idea, but I'm not sure I can keep it in."

"Babe, let's go out tonight, just you and me. That way, we can celebrate without letting the news slip. I'll call Jessica, and she and George can have a magical merry Monday while we go have dinner at River Watch," I suggest.

"That sounds great! I can already taste the maple Manhattan and apple cider salmon. How do you feel after your massage?" Alan, always caring about my pain.

"I actually feel pretty good. I'm going to head to the gym, and then I'll come home and get ready for dinner."

"Sounds good," Alan says. "Kate?"

"Yes, Alan?"

"I love you."

"I love you too, Alan."

*****

GIVING INN

Christmas Morning

As the family sits on the floor, opening their stockings and munching on their traditional Christmas morning Pop-Tarts, I eagerly await the opening of the presents under the tree. Specifically, the new one we just put under for George.

Jessica gets up to play Santa, as we call it. She places each person present in front of them until a mound is made and everyone's gifts are distributed. Jessica has played this role since she could tell whose gifts were whose.

I insist that George opens the newest gift last. We all go around opening the thoughtfully picked and purchased trinkets, gadgets, and toys. Finally, everyone had opened all their gifts except George's final gift.

"Go ahead, George," Alan says. "Open it."

George rips open the wrapping paper to reveal a basketball jacket with the name BROWN embroidered on the back and George embroidered on the front.

"Wow! That's really cool! But why does it have your last name on it?"

"Because it's your last name too, George," Jessica says.

"George, we got approved to start the adoption process. You are going to officially be a Brown," I add.

"And George, you never have to go back to the boy's home again," Alan states.

"Yahoo!" George yells as he jumps into our arms and gives us a hug so big it knocks us over, and we all lay on the floor laughing—so full of joy and gratitude.

The last few months have been such a whirlwind, from losing Molly to my health issues to meeting George, but I can say that life has not been boring—hard but not boring. Through all of this, though life may not be perfect, I see God's hand in my life. Even though not everything is resolved, I'm grateful. I'm so, so grateful He answered the prayers of a sweet little boy, and because of that, my heart is fuller than I could have imagined. I know I have a long road ahead of me. Donald, my investor, called yesterday to talk about a new inn. I'm not sure that's the route I'll take this time. For this moment right now, I'm so very content to just be in the little town of Alexandria Bay with my sweet family and my two busy inns. God is good.

> And we know that God causes everything to work together for the good of those who love Him and are called according to His purpose for them. (Romans 8:28)

Chapter 9

Five years later

"You look so beautiful, Jessica," I say as I dab my eyes. No time to touch up my makeup today; besides, this is her day.

"Thanks, Mom. Are you sure it's not going to rain today?" She asks for the fourteenth time as she peeks out the window to the garden in the back of the inn.

The gazebo was freshly cleaned with crystal stars hanging from the inside along with the gazebo's usual dress of twinkle lights along the outside and running up the columns. Wisteria was in full bloom, draping down around the outside of the gazebo like a beautiful flower crown.

The light slowly expands, and the afternoon arrives. As I open the window, the perfumed aroma of hyacinths floats on the fresh April breeze. Rose pink and snow-white blossoms scatter along the lawn. Vibrant tulips sprout profusely as spring's subtle awakening makes way for a time-honored tradition.

The cherry blossom trees were in full bloom as well, to make this a perfect spring wedding. Luckily, they are far enough away from the chairs, so no one will have blossoms raining down on their heads during the ceremony or reception. Who needs to catch a bouquet if they have a plate full of cherry blossoms?

Speaking of the bride's bouquet, Jessica chose to compliment blooms of lilacs, pink ranunculus, white chamomile, and sprigs of eucalyptus. It looks beautiful in the garden. The guests sitting in their spring hues also look amazing in the garden. The garden of Paradise Inn was made for spring weddings.

"Jessica," I say softly. "It's time."

I gather the train of her dress and help her make her way downstairs. I can't believe my little girl is getting married. The little girl who dressed up as Tinkerbell and Princess Sophia. The little girl who sang at the top of her lungs and played with her ponies for hours. The little girl who made me a mom is now becoming a wife.

Alan wipes at the tears pouring out of his eyes as Jessica links her arm to his. I step in front of them, and George leads me to my seat. He looks so dashing in his tuxedo. He takes his job as an usher at his big sister's wedding very seriously. As I take my seat, the procession starts. Everyone stands to watch as Alan walks our beautiful Jessica down the aisle.

This may be the ending of one story, but it's the beginning of the next.

The end

Toffee Coffee Cake Crumble

Streusel
- 1 3/4 cups flour
- 1 cup light brown sugar
- 1 1/4 tsp ground cinnamon
- 1/4 tsp salt
- 3/4 cup (1 1/2 sticks) unsalted butter

Cake
- 1/2 cup butter softened
- 2 cups flour
- 1 1/4 tsp baking powder
- 1/2 tsp baking soda
- 1/2 tsp salt
- 1 cup of granulated sugar
- 2 large eggs
- 1 1/2 tsp vanilla
- 1 cup sour cream
- 1/2 cup of toffee bits/chips

Instructions: Preheat oven to 350 degrees Fahrenheit. I use Pam baking spray to grease a 9×13 pan (trust me, I made the mistake of using an 8×8, and I'm still cleaning up the bottom of my oven!)

Streusel: Add flour, sugar, cinnamon, salt, and butter to a small mixing bowl. Using a pastry cutter, fork, or your hands, then mix until it forms pea-sized clumps. Refrigerate.

Cake: Add dry ingredients (flour, baking powder, baking soda, and salt) and whisk to combine. Set aside for now. In a large bowl, beat together the butter and sugar until fluffy. Beat in one egg at a time. Beat in vanilla extract. Add 1/3 of the flour mixture. Beat together. Add in 1/3 of the sour cream. Beat together. Continue these steps two more times until everything is incorporated and blended well. Fold in toffee chips.

Add half the cake batter to the prepared pan, spreading evenly. Add half of the refrigerated streusel, spreading in an even layer. Top with remaining cake batter, then add the last half of the streusel on top. Next, sprinkle another 1/2 cup of toffee bits on top of the streusel. Bake for fifty-five minutes. The top should be golden brown, and when a toothpick is inserted into the center, it should come out clean or have a few moist crumbs.

Remove from the oven, let cool on a wire rack, and enjoy with a cup of your favorite coffee!

About the Author

Kathy Branning was born and raised in Southern California. Kathy has been a published author for four years. She and her family are living in New York City following the fall of God on their life.

Kathy uses her writing to process grief, explore dreams, and experience and share hope and healing with her readers.

Kathy considers her faith and family to be most important to her. You can almost always find her having coffee or serving a meal to friends and family. *Giving Inn* is the third and final book in the *Tales of an Innkeeper* series. This sequel to book 2, It's an Inn-side Job, and book 1, 'Tis so Suite.

Printed in the USA
CPSIA information can be obtained
at www.ICGtesting.com
CBHW022109291124
18172CB00029B/391